First published in 2015 by
Hodder Children's Books
This paperback edition published in 2016

Text © Mij Kelly 2015
Illustrations © Holly Clifton-Brown 2015

Hodder Children's Books
An imprint of Hachette Children's Group
Part of Hodder & Stoughton
Carmelite House
50 Victoria Embankment
London EC4Y 0DZ

ISBN: 978 1 444 90607 3
10 9 8 7 6 5 4 3 2 1

Printed in China

An Hachette UK Company
www.hachette.co.uk

Hodder
Children's
Books

WHO puts the

ANIMALS to BED?

MIJ KELLY and HOLLY CLIFTON-BROWN

At the end of the day,
at the start of the night,
when the earth is half dark,
when the sky is half light,

who puts the
animals to bed?

Who helps the cat
down from the shed?

Who finds the bear
that went astray
and quiets the dog
that wants to play?

Who picks the downy duckling up

and soothes the yawning sea-lion pup?

Who blows the crocodile a kiss

and asks the snake - please - not to hiss,

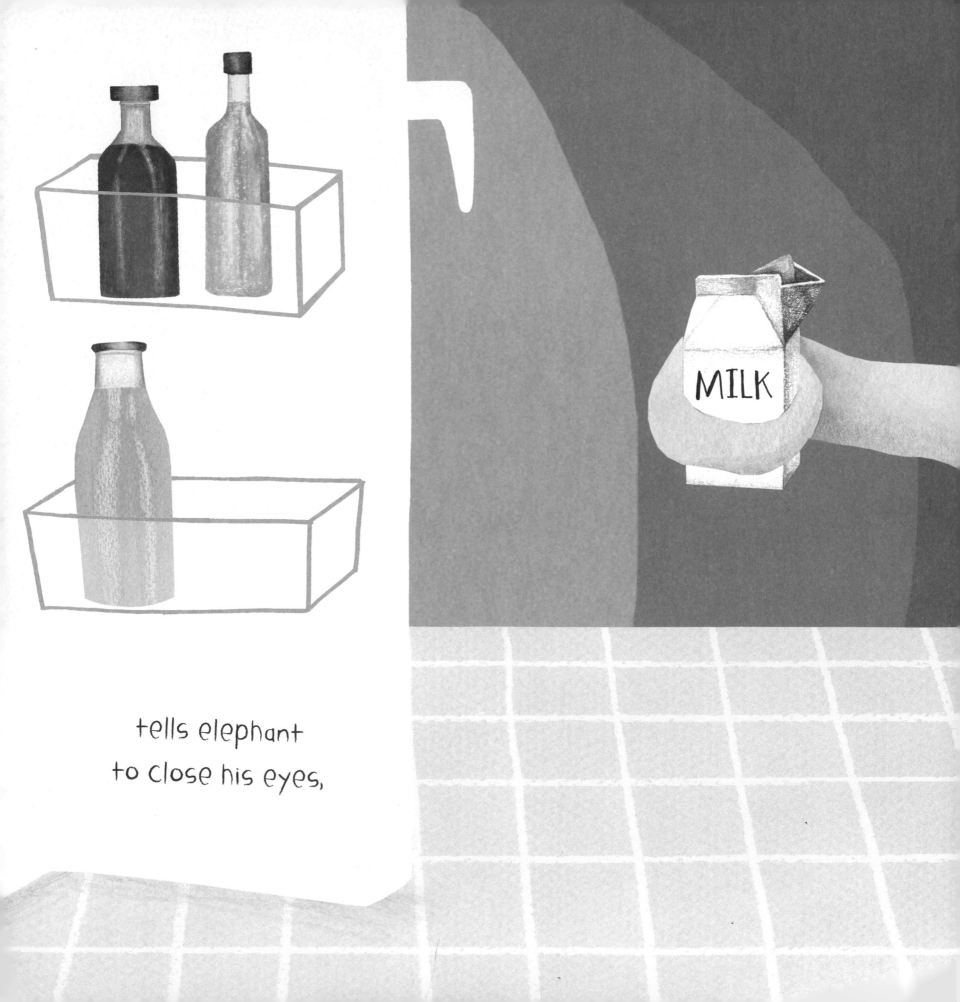

tells elephant
to close his eyes,

and sings the lion a lullaby?

When tawny owl goes:

"Twit-too-woo,"

who whispers:
"Hush?"

Oh tell me who
strokes the tired
old tiger's head?
Who puts the
animals to bed?

Is it you? Is it you?
Well, snuggle down too,

with your lion and your
bear, or your kangaroo,

with rabbit and monkey,
penguin and dog,
gorilla and turtle,
or maybe with frog.

Give them all a big hug
and turn down the light

and with the whole wide, wild world
sleep in peace for the night.

Other **great** titles to share together by Mij Kelly:

WILLIAM and the NIGHT-TRAIN
Mij Kelly and Alison Jay

Friendly Day
MIJ KELLY CHARLES FUGE

MARY McQUILLAN MIJ KELLY
Atchoo!
The Complete Guide to Good Manners

MIJ KELLY Have you seen my Potty?
MARY McQUILLAN

A BED OF YOUR OWN
MIJ KELLY AND MARY McQUILLAN

NURSERY TIME
MIJ KELLY MARY McQUILLAN

For fun activities, further information and to order, visit www.hodderchildrens.co.uk